Artful Reading

Bob Raczka

D1361555

MILLBROOK PRESS / MINNEAPOLIS

Families Reading Together
Palm Beach County
LIBRARY
www.pbclibrary.org System
Dream. Discover. Do.

To Larry & Nancy, two of my favorite book lovers,
with thanks for your enthusiastic support

Text copyright © 2008 by Bob Raczka

All rights reserved. International copyright secured. No part of this book may be reproduced, stored in a retrieval system, or transmitted in any form or by any means—electronic, mechanical, photocopying, recording, or otherwise—without the prior written permission of Lerner Publishing Group, Inc., except for the inclusion of brief quotations in an acknowledged review.

Millbrook Press
A division of Lerner Publishing Group, Inc.
241 First Avenue North
Minneapolis, MN 55401 U.S.A.

Website address: www.lernerbooks.com

Library of Congress Cataloging-in-Publication Data

Raczka, Bob.
Artful reading / by Bob Raczka.
p. cm.
ISBN: 978–0–8225–6754–7 (lib. bdg. : alk. paper)
1. Reading in art—Juvenile literature. 2. Painting, Modern—Juvenile literature. I. Title.
ND1460.R42R33 2008
700′.557—dc22 2006035083

Manufactured in the United States of America
3 – DP – 7/1/11

Cover art courtesy of: © 2007 Estate of Pablo Picasso/Artists Rights Society (ARS), New York. Pablo Picasso, Spanish, 1881–1973, *Two Girls Reading* 1934, oil on canvas, 92.2 cm x 73 cm (36 5/16 in. x 28 3/4 in.), Gift of The Carey Walker Foundation 1994/1.67, University of Michigan Museum of Art.

Interior art courtesy of: Page 3: Museum Ludwig, Repro: Rheinisches Bildarchiv Köln; Page 4: Smithsonian American Art Museum, Washington, DC/Art Resource, NY; Page 5: The Metropolitan Museum of Art, Bequest of Sam A. Lewisohn, 1951. (51.112.3) Photograph by Malcom Varon. Photograph © 1979 The Metropolitan Museum of Art; Page 6: Glasgow City Council (Museums), Edgar Degas, *Edmond Duranty*; Page 7: Victoria & Albert Museum, London/Art Resource, NY; Page 8: Paul Cézanne, *The Artist's Father, Reading "L'Événement"*, Collection of Mr. and Mrs. Paul Mellon, Image © Board of Trustees, National Gallery of Art, Washington DC; Page 9: Réunion des Musées Nationaux/Art Resource, NY; Page 10: Jean-Honoré Fragonard, *A Young Girl Reading*, Gift of Mrs. Mellon Bruce in memory of her father, Andrew W. Mellon, Image © Board of Trustees, National Gallery of Art, Washington DC; Page 11: Scala/Art Resource, NY; Page 12–13: Edouard Manet, *The Railway*, Gift of Horace Havemeyer in memory of his mother, Louisine W. Havemeyer, Image © Board of Trustees, National Gallery of Art, Washington DC; Page 14: Woman Reading a Letter, c.1662–63 (oil on canvas), Vermeer, Jan (1632–75) © Rijksmuseum, Amsterdam, Holland/The Bridgeman Art Library; Page 15: Mary Cassatt, American, 1844–1926, *On a Balcony*, 1878/79, oil on canvas, 89.9 x 65.2 cm, Gift of Mrs. Albert J. Beveridge in memory of her aunt, Delia Spencer Field, 1938.18, The Art Institute of Chicago. Photography © The Art Institute of Chicago; Page 16: © National Gallery Collection; By kind permission of the Trustees of the National Gallery, London/CORBIS; Page 17: © 2007 Succession H. Matisse, Paris/Artists Rights Society (ARS), New York. Photograph © The Barnes Foundation, Merion Station, Pennsylvania/CORBIS; Page 18–19: Bildarchiv Pressischer Kulturbesitz/Art Resource, NY; Page 20: Réunion des Musées Nationaux/Art Resource, NY; Page 21: © Geoffrey Clements/CORBIS; Page 22–23: © 2007 Milton Avery Trust/Artists Rights Society (ARS), New York. Photograph © Terra Foundation for American Art, Chicago/Art Resource, NY; Page 24: © National Gallery Collection; By kind permission of the Trustees of the National Gallery, London/CORBIS; Page 25: Reproduced with the kind permission of the Earl of Pembroke and the Trustees of the Wilton Estate; Page 26: Courtesy of the Milwaukee Public Library; Page 27: © 2007 Estate of Pablo Picasso/Artists Rights Society (ARS), New York. Pablo Picasso, Spanish, 1881–1973, *Two Girls Reading* 1934, oil on canvas, 92.2 cm x 73 cm (36 5/16 in. x 28 3/4 in.), Gift of The Carey Walker Foundation 1994/1.67, University of Michigan Museum of Art; Page 28–29: © 2007 The Jacob and Gwendolyn Lawrence Foundation, Seattle/Artist Rights Society (ARS), New York. Photograph © Smithsonian American Art Museum, Washington, DC/Art Resource, NY.

Read by yourself.

August Macke • *Man Reading in the Park* (1914) • Museum Ludwig, Cologne, Germany

Read with each other.

Charles Willson Peale • *Mrs. James Smith and Grandson* (1776)
Smithsonian American Art Museum, Washington, D.C.

Read one good book.
Then read another.

Vincent Van Gogh • *L'Arlésienne: Madame Joseph-Michel Ginoux* (1888 or 1889)
Metropolitan Museum of Art, New York

Read to discover what something means.

Edgar Degas • *Portrait of Edmond Duranty* (1879) • Glasgow Museums and Art Galleries

Read to escape to a place you can dream.

Dante Gabriel Rossetti • *The Day Dream* (1880) • Victoria and Albert Museum, London

Read the news.

Paul Cézanne • *The Artist's Father* (1866) • National Gallery of Art, Washington, D.C.

Or read a globe.

Johannes Vermeer • *The Astronomer* (1668) • Musée du Louvre, Paris

Read in a dress.

Jean-Honoré Fragonard • *A Young Girl Reading* (ca. 1776) • National Gallery of Art, Washington, D.C.

Or read in your robe.

Albrecht Dürer • *The Four Apostles (John & Peter)* (1523–26) • Alte Pinakothek, Munich

Édouard Manet • *The Railway* (1873) • National Gallery of Art, Washington, D.C.

Read while you wait for your train to come in.

Read to find out how somebody's been.

Johannes Vermeer • *Woman in Blue Reading a Letter* (1662–63) • Rijksmuseum, Amsterdam

Read in a garden.

Mary Cassatt • *On a Balcony* (1878–79) • Art Institute of Chicago

Read in a house.

Antonello da Messina • *St. Jerome in His Study* (ca. 1475) • The National Gallery, London

Read by the window.

Henri Matisse • *The French Window at Nice* (1919) • Barnes Foundation, Merion, Pennsylvania

Pierre-Auguste Renoir • *Children's Afternoon at Wargemont* (1884)
Staatliche Museen zu Berlin

Read
on the
couch.

Read while you work.

Quentin Massys • *The Moneylender and His Wife* (1514) • Musée du Louvre, Paris

Read while you ride.

Edward Hopper • *Compartment C, Car 293* (1938) • IBM Corporation, Armonk, New York

Milton Avery • *Adolescence* (1947) • Terra Foundation for American Art, Chicago

Read what you want. It's for you to decide.

Read when you're young.

Jean-Baptiste-Siméon Chardin • *Young Schoolmistress* (ca. 1735–36) • The National Gallery, London

Read when you're old.

Attributed to Rembrandt van Rijn • *Rembrandt's Mother* (1629) • Wilton House, Salisbury, UK

Read all the words
you can possibly hold.

Carl Spitzweg • *The Bookworm* (1850) • Milwaukee Public Library

Read to a friend. That's what friends are for.

Pablo Picasso • *Two Girls Reading* (1934) • University of Michigan Museum of Art, Ann Arbor

Jacob Lawrence • *The Library* (1960) • Smithsonian American Art Museum, Washington, D.C.

Read all your life and you'll never be bored.

ARTISTS AS READERS AND WRITERS

August Macke
(1887–1914) German
To spread new ideas about art, August Macke and a group of his friends published a special book called *Der Blaue Reiter* (The Blue Rider) almanac. It was a collection of artwork and essays on art from all over Europe.

Charles Willson Peale
(1741–1827) American
The boy in this painting, whose name is Campbell Smith, is reading a book called *The Art of Speaking*. His finger is pointing to the words "To be, or not to be" from William Shakespeare's famous play, *Hamlet*.

Vincent Van Gogh
(1853–1890) Dutch
Vincent Van Gogh was a great lover of books. He read everything from the plays of William Shakespeare to the fairy tales of Hans Christian Andersen. One of his favorite books was *A Christmas Carol* by Charles Dickens.

Edgar Degas
(1834–1917) French
Edmond Duranty was a good friend of Edgar Degas. Duranty was a novelist, but none of his books ever became very popular. He was also an art critic who wrote favorably about Degas and the other Impressionists.

Dante Gabriel Rossetti
(1828–1882) English
Dante Rossetti was a poet as well as a painter. He grew up in London, and as a boy, he spent many hours in the British Museum Reading Room, absorbing as much great literature as he could.

Paul Cézanne
(1839–1906) French
Because Paul Cézanne's father was a banker, he read a newspaper that was popular with businessmen. But as a little joke, Cézanne painted him reading *L'Evenement*, the newspaper preferred by French artists and writers.

Johannes Vermeer
(1632–1675) Dutch
The globe that Johannes Vermeer's astronomer is reading is a globe of the stars, called a celestial globe. This one was made by the famous Dutch globemaker and mapmaker Jodocus Hondius in the year 1600.

Jean-Honoré Fragonard
(1732–1806) French
Today we consider Jean Fragonard to be one of the greatest painters of his time. But for many years after he died in 1806, he was forgotten. In fact, he wasn't even mentioned in a history of art that was published in 1873.

Albrecht Dürer
(1471–1528) German
In addition to making art, Albrecht Dürer also wrote several books about it. The final three volumes of his "Four Books on Human Proportion," which he worked on all his life, were finally published six months after he died.

Antonello da Messina
(ca.1430–1479) Sicilian
Saint Jerome is considered one of the four fathers of the Catholic Church. As da Messina shows us, Saint Jerome is famous for translating the Bible from Hebrew and Aramaic into Latin. This version of the Bible is called the Vulgate.

Édouard Manet
(1832–1883) French
One of Édouard Manet's friends, Stéphane Mallarmé, was a poet. Mallarmé did not become well known until he published a translation of Edgar Allan Poe's famous poem, "The Raven." The poem was illustrated by Manet.

Henri Matisse
(1869–1954) French
Henri Matisse wrote and illustrated a book called *Jazz*, which was published in 1947, when he was seventy-seven years old. He illustrated it with colorful cut-paper collages, and the text is in his own handwriting.

Johannes Vermeer
(1632–1675) Dutch
During his lifetime, Johannes Vermeer (also known as Jan) completed very few paintings. In fact, only thirty-five of his confirmed works have survived to this day. But of those paintings, seven show women reading or writing letters.

Pierre-Auguste Renoir
(1841–1919) French
Renoir and his wife Aline had three children, all of them boys. Jean, their second son, became a successful filmmaker. In 1962 he wrote a touching biography of his father called *Renoir, My Father*.

Mary Cassatt
(1844–1926) American
Mary Cassatt often used her sister, Lydia, as a model for her paintings. In 2001 the author Harriet Scott Chessman published a novel about Mary's relationship with her sister called *Lydia Cassatt Reading the Morning Paper*.

Quentin Massys
(also spelled Messys)
(1466–1530) Belgian
The moneylender's wife, who is turning the pages of a religious book, is not the only person reading in this painting. If you look closely at the mirror on the table, you can see the reflection of a man reading by a window.

Edward Hopper
(1882–1967) American
The theme of Edward Hopper's work seems to be loneliness. He often painted people reading, lost in their own little worlds—just as we get lost in our own little worlds when we look at his paintings.

Milton Avery
(1885–1965) American
Milton Avery was a great family man, and he often entertained his wife, Sally, and their daughter, March, by reading out loud to them. His favorite authors included Herman Melville and Henry David Thoreau.

Jean-Baptiste-Siméon Chardin
(1699–1779) French
Because Jean Chardin painted scenes from everyday life, many of them were made into engravings and sold to the public. The engravings often came with poems, which were written by the engravers to "explain" the pictures.

Rembrandt Harmenszoon van Rijn (ca. 1606–1669) Dutch
There is controversy as to whether Rembrandt actually painted this portrait. Current scholars think the master may have rendered the Bible but that it was mainly painted by Rembrandt's friend Jan Lievens.

Carl Spitzweg
(1808–1885) German
Ever since Carl Spitzweg painted *The Bookworm*, engravings and posters of it have been popular among people who love to read. Appropriately enough, the original painting now hangs in the Milwaukee Public Library.

Pablo Picasso
(1881–1973) Spanish
According to the *Guinness Book of World Records*, Pablo Picasso produced more paintings than any other artist ever known–about 13,500 in all. He also created nearly 34,000 book illustrations.

Jacob Lawrence
(1917–2000) American
The library was an important place to Jacob Lawrence. As a boy, he learned to paint at the Harlem Art Workshop, which was located inside the New York Public Library. Later, he used the library to do research for his paintings.